A CAMEL
IN THE TENT

TO HELEN
AND
JOHN

A CAMEL
IN THE TENT

RETOLD BY KATHERINE EVANS

Illustrated by the Author

ALBERT WHITMAN & COMPANY • CHICAGO

Published simultaneously in
the Dominion of Canada by
George J. McLeod Ltd., Toronto
Lithographed in the U.S.A.

Once long ago, there was a rich sultan who
lived in a palace in a far-away city called Taza.

The sultan had eight beautiful daughters.

He loved them all dearly and did everything he could to make them happy.

This was not easy. All they thought of day in and day out were jewels and fine clothes.

They were not satisfied with the simple dresses and plain shoes that could be bought for them in Taza.

One day, the sultan sent a message to Mohammed, the very best merchant of Fez.

He ordered fine silk dresses of many colors and coats embroidered in gold. He ordered soft leather slippers of red, yellow and green and jewels of gold and coral.

The eight beautiful daughters were very happy. They could hardly wait for the day when Mohammed would bring all these wonderful things across the desert from Fez to Taza.

In the market place in Fez the time came
when all the work was done. The last little
shoe had its turned-up toe embroidered. All the
veils and robes were hemmed and trimmed.
The jewels were polished and packed in cases.

Mohammed was well pleased with his work.
"These will make their eyes shine," he said
to his workers as they packed everything away.
"Such beautiful things are not to be found
in far-away Taza."

Early in the morning, Mohammed called for his camel. Onto the camel's back, he tied the trunks and cases and things for the trip.

Then he climbed up onto the high hump and set off across the desert to Taza.

After a while, the sun grew burning hot. Mohammed put up his red silk umbrella.

Just before he reached Taza, the sun went
down. The wind began to blow and it was
very cold.

Mohammed put up his tent. He took the
trunks and cases inside with him. It was cozy
and warm and soon Mohammed went to sleep.

Before long, he was awakened by loud groans and moans outside the tent.

"What is the matter out there?" he called.

"Oh, Master, I cannot sleep," said the camel. "All day I carried you across the desert and now I am tired. The wind blows so cold out here. Please just let me put my head in your tent."

"It is true that you carried me on your back all day and deserve to rest. Put your head inside my tent," said the merchant.

So the camel put his head inside the tent and Mohammed went back to sleep.

In a short while, the camel began to moan and groan again.

"My legs are cold and stiff from walking all day across the desert. Please let me put my front legs in your tent. Then I can go to sleep."

Mohammed was only half awake.

"Yes, yes, you have walked far," he said. "Put your front legs inside the tent and we will both go to sleep."

The camel put his front legs inside the tent and Mohammed went back to sleep.

Soon the camel said, "I cannot rest. My head
and front legs are warm but my hump and back
legs are cold. Master, may I put them inside
your tent? Then I will be able to sleep."

Mohammed was so sleepy, he just said "Yes."
Now the camel had his head and front legs
and hump and back legs all inside the tent.

It was a small tent and after the camel was inside he said to himself, "There is not room in here for all these trunks and cases."

So he pushed and pushed and pushed them all out. He had pushed so hard that the trunks opened. The wind blew away all the beautiful dresses and robes and little slippers. The jewels were being covered by the sand.

Still the camel was not comfortable. "Both of us can never sleep in this tent," he said to himself. "The master will have to go."

So he pushed and pushed again until he pushed Mohammed out into the cold night. Then at last the camel was comfortable and he went to sleep.

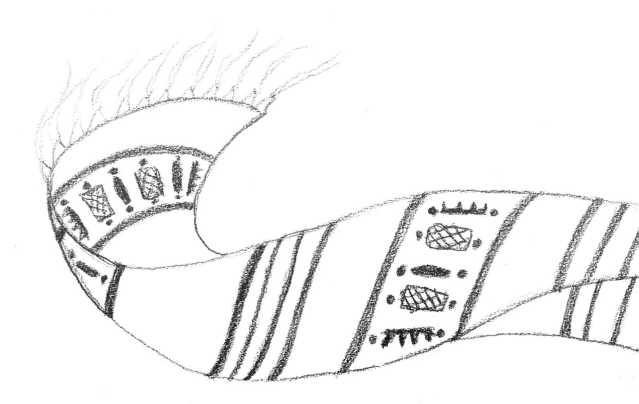

Mohammed awoke and found himself outside
the tent. When he saw that almost all the clothes
had blown away and the jewels were nowhere
to be found, he cried, "Allah, have mercy! What
will the sultan say to me?"

Mohammed went to the palace in Taza. He told the sultan that everything had blown away and he had nothing but empty trunks.

The eight beautiful daughters were very unhappy. They wept and wailed as though their hearts would break. This made the sultan very angry.

But Mohammed promised the daughters he
would go back to Fez and make even more
beautiful dresses than before.

He promised such wonderful things that the daughters dried their tears.

So the sultan forgave Mohammed and said
to him:

"After this, do not let a camel get his
head in your tent. For when you give the
foolish a little, they want too much."

JEFFERSON